David Ross Locke

Hannah Jane

David Ross Locke

Hannah Jane

ISBN/EAN: 9783743301108

Manufactured in Europe, USA, Canada, Australia, Japa

Cover: Foto ©Andreas Hilbeck / pixelio.de

Manufactured and distributed by brebook publishing software
(www.brebook.com)

David Ross Locke

Hannah Jane

HANNAH JAN

BY

DAVID ROSS LO

EX LIBRIS

"The great house crowded full of guests."

HANNAH JANE

BY

DAVID ROSS LOCKE

(Petroleum V. Nasby)

ILLUSTRATED

BOSTON
LEE AND SHEPARD PUBLISHERS
NEW YORK CHARLES T. DILLINGHAM
1882

University Press: John Wilson & Son,
Cambridge.

LIST OF ILLUSTRATIONS.

Designed by

S. G. McCUTCHEON and E. H. GARRETT.

Arranged and Engraved

By GEORGE T. ANDREW.

HANNAH JANE.

She isn't half so handsome as when, twenty years agone,
At her old home in Piketon Parson Avery made us one;
The great house crowded full of guests of high and low
      degree,
The girls all envying Hannah Jane, the boys all envy-
      ing me.

Her fingers then were taper, and her skin was white as
    milk.
Her brown hair — what a mass it was! and soft and fine
    as silk :
No wind-moved willow by a brook had ever such a grace :
The form of Aphrodite, with a pure Madonna face.

She had but meagre schooling : her little notes to me
Were full of crooked pot-hooks, and the worst orthog-
    raphy.
Her "dear" she spelled with double *e*, and "kiss" with
    single *s :*
But when one's crazed with passion, what's a letter more
    or less?

She blundered in her writing, and she blundered when
    she spoke,
And ev'ry rule of syntax that old Murray made she broke;
But she was fresh and beautiful, and I—well, I was young:
Her form and face far, far outweighed the blunders of
    her tongue.

I was but little better. True, I'd longer been at school;
My tongue and pen were run, perhaps, a trifle more by
    rule;
But that was all: the neighbors round, who knew us
    through and through,
Spoke but the truth in calling her the better of the two.

How changed she is! the light of youth has faded from
   her eyes;
Her wavy hair is gone — that loss the coiffeur's art
   supplies;
Her form is thin and angular; she slightly forward bends;
Her fingers, once so shapely, now are stumpy at the ends.

She has made but little progress, and in little are we one;
The beauty rare that more than hid that great defect
   is gone.
My well-to-do relations now deride my homely wife,
And pity me that I am tied to such a clod for life.

I know there is a difference: at reception and levée
The brightest, wittiest, and most famed of women smile
       on me;
And everywhere I hold my place among the greatest men;
And sometimes sigh, with Whittier's judge, "Alas! it
       might have been."

When they all crowd around me, stately dames and
      brilliant belles,
And yield to me the homage that all great success compels,
Discussing art and state-craft, and literature as well,
From Homer down to Thackeray, and Swedenborg on
      " Hell,"

I can't forget that from these streams my wife has never
      quaffed,
Has never with Ophelia wept, nor with Jack Falstaff
      laughed;
Of authors, actors, artists — why, she hardly knows the
      names;
She slept while I was speaking on the *Alabama* claims.

I can't forget ——   Just at this point another form
        appears, —
The wife I wedded as she was before my prosperous years;
I travel o'er the dreary road we journeyed side by side,
And wonder what my share would be if Justice should
        divide.

She had four hundred dollars from her father's old estate;
On that we two were married, and bravely faced our fate.
I wrestled with my books; her task was harder far than
        mine —
'Twas to make two hundred dollars do the work for us
        of nine.

At last I was admitted; then I had my legal lore,
An office with a stove and desk, and books perhaps a
    score;
She had her beauty and her youth, and some housewifely
    skill,
And love for me and faith in me, and back of that a will.

I had no friends behind me — no influence to aid;
I worked and fought for every precious inch of ground
    I made,
And how she fought beside me! never woman lived on
    less;
In two long years she never spent a single cent for dress.

Ah! how she cried for joy when my first legal fight was
  won,
When our eclipse passed partly by, and we could see the
  sun!
The fee was fifty dollars — 'twas the work of half a year —
First captive, lean and scraggy, of my legal bow and spear.

I well remember, when my coat (the only one I had)
Was seedy grown and threadbare, and, in fact, most
  "shocking bad,"
The tailor's stern remark when I a modest order made:
" Cash is the basis, Sir, on which we tailors do our trade."

Her winter cloak was in his shop by noon that very day;
She wrought on hickory shirts at night that tailor's bill
to pay.
I got a coat, and wore it; but alas! poor Hannah Jane,
Ne'er went to church or lecture till warm weather came
again.

Our second season she refused a cloak of any sort,
That I might have a decent suit in which t' appear in
court;
She made her last year's bonnet do that I might have
a hat:
Talk of the old-time martyrs, flame-enveloped, after that!

No negro ever worked so hard: a servant's pay to save,
She made herself most willingly a household drudge and
slave.
What wonder that she never read a magazine or book,
Combining as she did in one, nurse, housemaid, seamstress,
cook!

What wonder that the beauty fled that once I so adored!
The rose and lily in her face my kitchen fire devoured;
Her plump, soft, rounded arm was once too fair to be
     concealed :
Hard work for me that softness into sinewy strength
     congealed.

I was her altar, and her love the sacrificial flame;
Ah! with what pure devotion she to that altar came,
And, tearful, flung thereon — alas! I did not know it
     then —
All that she was, and more than that, all that she might
     have been!

At last I won a grand success! our lives then parted wide;
I swiftly climbed the rising road, she walked not by my
    side.
I'd tried my speed and mettle, gained strength in every
    race ;
Far up the heights of life was I — she drudging at the base.

She made me take the stump each fall; she said 'twas my
    career:
And wild applause of list'ning crowds was music to my
    ear.
What stimulus had she to cheer her dreary solitude?
For me she lived on gladly in a weary widowhood.

She couldn't hear my maiden speech, but when the press
    agreed
'Twas the best one of the season, those comments she
    could read ;
And with a gush of pride thereat, which I had never felt,
She sent them to me in a note, with half the words
    misspelt.

I to the legislature went, and said that she should go
To see the busy world with me, and what 'twas doing know.
With tearful smile she answered, "No! four dollars is
      the pay;
The Bates House rates for board *for one* is just that
      sum per day."

At twenty-eight the State-house; on the bench at thirty-
      three;
At forty every gate in life was opened wide to me.
I nursed my powers, and grew, and made my point; but
      she —
Bearing such weary pack-horse loads, what could the
      woman be?

What could she be! Oh, shame! I blush to think what
    she has been:
The most unselfish of all wives to the selfishest of men.
Yes, plain and homely now she is; she's ignorant, 'tis
    true:
For me she rubbed herself quite out: I represent the two.

Well, I suppose that I might do as other men have done—
First break her heart with cold neglect, then shove her
    out alone.
The world would say 'twas well, and more, would give
    great praise to me
For having borne with "such a wife" so uncomplainingly.

And shall I? No! The contract 'twixt Hannah, God,
      and me
Was not for one or twenty years, but for eternity.
No matter what the world may think; I know down in
      my heart
If either, I'm delinquent: she has bravely done her part.

There's another world beyond this; and on the final day
Will intellect and learning against such devotion weigh?
And when the one made of us two, is torn apart again,
I'll kick the beam, for God is just, and He knows Hannah
      Jane.